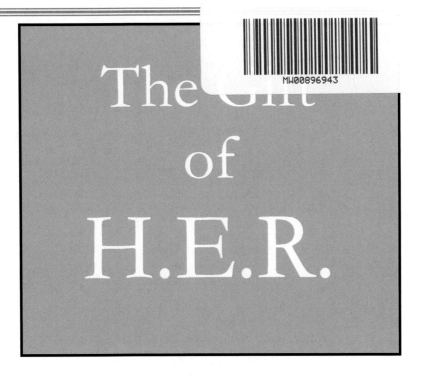

The Gift of H.E.R.

Pearls

of

Hope, Emergence, and Resolve

The original prose, poetry & quotes
of

Timid Masses

Pencil Me In Publications, LLC
5810 Kingstowne Ctr #120-108
Alexandria, VA 22315

Printed in the United States of America
First Printing, 2020
ISBN: 9781081196646

www.TimidMasses.com

Royalty free illustrations, photos and graphics courtesy of
Pixabay, https://pixabay.com/ and
Pexels, https://pexels.com

Dedicated to the last angel that fell to earth.

- Timid Masses

Table of Contents

Foreword

We ordinarily think of pearls as the fine jewelry worn across a woman's nape or inlaid into an artistic piece to enhance its aesthetics. But pearls also have a secondary meaning. Pearls can represent bits of wisdom and knowledge that a person holds in high regard and assigns considerable value to its possession. The Gift of HER is intended to provide insights and stimulate conversations regarding the concept of inner beauty.

What makes a person beautiful? Beauty has invariably been at the discretion of the beholder. Each person embraces their own way of defining what beauty is and what is acceptable as beautiful. Very often beauty is mistaken for well placed physical characteristics, but beauty is considerably deeper than what can be seen. At its core, beauty engenders a feeling of euphoria. A feeling of uniqueness and rarity. A transitioning from the ordinary to the extraordinary.

The Gift of HER is a poetic commentary that attempts to capture the challenges women face each day combatting societal pressures that shape and define what it means to be a woman and what it means to be beautiful. It explores the various shapes and hues, thoughts and attitudes that form her core. No man can ever completely comprehend what it means to be a woman. But if we show her love and affection; give her support and understanding; and gift her with the very best of ourselves that we have to offer, then we will begin to appreciate the importance of her to our lives. And, the significant role she plays with making our world more beautiful.

Timid Masses

Sensationally

I will love you sensationally,

but first you have to love me.

I will hold you so close that you can hear my heart beat,

but first you must hold me.

I will breathe life into your lungs through my kiss,

speak sweet words into each of your ears that you cannot resist.

Make you feel like the king you are meant to be.

But before I do any of that for you,

there is something you must do for me;

love me sensationally.

Her Essence

Every woman has it inside of her,

it is what makes her special,

it is the source of her pride.

It dictates her attitude

at a given time or at a given place.

It chooses the clothes she wears

and determines what emotions are shown on her face.

When she moves, it moves with her.

She takes it everywhere she goes.

It covers her entire body,

from her head to her toes.

The swing of her hips when she walks.

The sweet tones of her voice when she talks.

The vibrancy you feel in her presence.

All because of her incredible essence.

How Much I Love You

Don't look back,
the past has got to pass.
Let it go, let it all go.
Memories hang from the ceiling like chandeliers,
whose crystal teardrops shimmer in the night,
when the light creeping into the room shines through their
transparency.
That's how it was with you, at first glance.
When your eyes surveyed the horizon to see if you could find me,
even though we never met.
Under the chandelier of the sky,
where stars form and light is born,
you wanted me, and I wanted you more.
So I extended my hand,
gently, subtly;
giving you a chance to escort me to the place you wanted me to go;
the place I have never been to before.
Without mincing words, my actions spoke loud and clear
—come closer dear, come near.
There are things I need to whisper in your ear
that only you should hear.
And when these words I speak reach into your soul,
compelling you to release your heart,
place your heart into my hands to hold.
It is then that you will know
how much I love you.

Unfurl

My emotions had me curled up.
Knotted in a ball of confusion trying to figure things out.
Attempting to grasp what this relationship was about.
Was it about you? Was it about me? Was it about us?

The impact of losing your love unnerved me
and made me question whether I wanted to live.
I curled up to fortify myself
to conceal my insides while I healed.

Don't mistake my curling up for lack of courage.
I am more courageous than you may think.
I handled your betrayal with dignity.
I learned how to survive,
how to embrace tomorrow,
how to stand on my own two feet.

I am prepared to come out now,
to climb up from the depths of misery.
I am prepared to let go of feelings I have held inside,
let go of you, let go of we.

Unencumbered by emotional anchors, I feel lifted, I feel free.
My mind rises to an elevation where the air is clear,
and I can unfurl and breathe.

Don't Mess With My Glory

Don't mess with the glory that rests upon my head.

It is the crown I wear when I go anywhere

and it has to be perfectly laid.

It's the first thing others notice about me.

It's the voice to my personal story.

It speaks to who I am

and how I should be received.

That's why I call it my glory.

So try not to stare at this crown I wear,

surely it will fill you with envy.

Keep your hands down,

don't you dare touch my hair.

Don't even think about messing with my glory.

Admire from afar,

stay right where you are and keep wishing you had my sheen.

My glory is royal, straight or curled,

it's the spectacular crown of a queen.

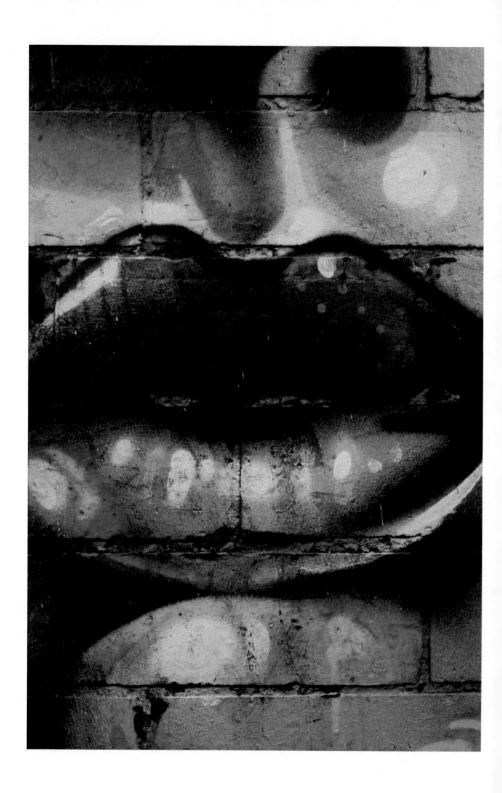

Will You Love Me As I Am?

I don't know how to be what I am not,

so will you love me as I am?

My eyes are the color of the fertile earth,

an exquisite ebony brown.

My hair I wear straight,

but my natural "glory" is curled at the crown.

My skin, sun-kissed,

radiates beneath my golden complexion.

My perfectly formed lips,

drip with the taste of the sweetest nectar.

Can you love me as I am?

Can you climb this mahogany tree

and rest comfortably in its arms?

I don't know how to be what I am not,

so will you love me as I am?

A Dynamic Woman

A dynamic woman is what I am,

it resonates deep within.

It hibernates in my thoughts,

lives at my core,

and is the catalyst of my inner strength.

It is the rhythm to my beating heart.

It is what sets me apart,

and raises me above the rest.

It elevates me to a place,

where I no longer accept second rate,

it's first or nothing else.

I wake each morning

prepared to leave my mark,

as I venture out the door.

My every move is life changing,

my positive attitude engaging,

filling my world with happiness and joy.

Don't try to stop me, just sit back and watch me.

When you see me, you will understand.

I am a dynamic woman, ready for the world,

and I know exactly who I am.

The Many Hues of Me

Colorful,

is the word I use to describe myself.

It means I am bright and vivacious, bold and tenacious,

I bring light to the world in which I live.

But if all you see is color,

then you haven't seen me, because there is so much more

I have inside to share.

Beneath the various hues and tints

are my thoughts, my hopes, and my dreams.

When I let my light shine

this color of mine, neither limits nor defines,

who I am or what I can be.

My Incredible Red Hat

I once owned a red hat,
that turned a head or two in its day.
I would wear it slanted on one side,
so it hides one eye,
then sashay upon my way.

Wherever I would go,
became a fashion show,
no one could look away.
All eyes were on me,
that's the way it's supposed to be,
when the red hat is on display.

Spectators looked on in awe,
not believing what they saw.
Men stared and women steamed.
All had to bow down when I came around,
acknowledging the presence of a queen.

I have yet to wear anything that dares,
to exude such a diva vibe.
Nothing yet, mimics the effects
of that incredible red hat of mine.

She Wants

A woman requires affection and care,

the same as she requires air.

A supple touch, a subtle gaze,

a heartfelt gesture given in an affectionate way.

A sweet word, whispered in her ear.

A soft kiss while holding her near.

She wants to feel comfortable in your arms.

She wants to feel safe and secure from harm.

She wants to see love reflected in your eyes,

as you fulfill her every dream

and make her fantasies come alive.

She wants to feel butterflies at the mention of your name,

feel flushed with passion as blood courses through her veins.

She wants to feel forever in the touch of your lips,

lose herself completely in your sensual kiss.

She wants to know your heart is faithful and true,

that the love you feel for her, matches the love she feels for you.

She wants you to appreciate her many complex ways,

and be with her through the years

as life counts down the days.

When the Sun Shines

When the sun shines, you just have to enjoy it.

Lay back and let it shine on you.

Bask in the warmth and splendor

as the day starts anew.

It doesn't matter who the rays touch first,

we all will enjoy it the same.

I have rather had the sunshine in my life,

then for my life to be filled with rain.

Let the cool breeze float pass you.

Let your worries sprout wings and fly away.

Let your smile be the sunshine,

when the sun sets upon the day.

An illuminating light,

radiant and bright,

stars envy your every move.

So the next time, you feel the sun shine,

relax and let it shine upon you!

Cinnamon Brown

I am proud to be,

in this cinnamon brown skin God chose for me.

There is nothing I would rather be

than wrapped entirely in ebony.

This complexion, that I wear.

Stretching from the roots of my hair to the bottom of my heels.

This hallow place where my soul lives,

causes chills to traverse my spine.

Makes others wish that they could switch,

so they can have skin like mine.

Make others turn to the sky and pray,

beseeching the touch that made me this way.

Begging, please permit me to become,

cinnamon brown by the kiss of the sun.

But they lack the melatonin infused in me,

that makes me a beautiful brown lady.

Dark as the sediments in the river Nile.

Brown as the Marula tree that grows in the wild.

Tan as African Opal carved from the ground.

I am proud to be cinnamon brown.

I Am

I am beautiful,

a vision to behold.

I am strong,

brave and bold.

I am intelligent,

I can articulate,

the feelings I have inside

and the thoughts that I think.

I am loving,

I believe in reciprocity.

I will give my love to you,

if you give your love to me.

I am supportive,

my heart and soul is fully invested.

I am faithful,

loyal, true, and tested.

I am royalty,

the descendant of a queen.

I am amazing, remarkable,

magnificent, dazzling,

I am

everything you ever dreamed.

34

Time For Change

Time for change,

time to rearrange some things in my life.

Release the anchors pinning me down.

elevate my thinking to new heights.

Spread the news for all to hear,

notify everyone that a metamorphosis is taking place.

I am surrounding myself with positivity,

cleansing myself of negative things.

I am anxious to embark on a new journey.

I've packed my bags and am prepared to go.

The next stop is into the universe,

into the darkness of the great unknown.

I am not going turning back.

I am not giving in to fear nor sadness.

For better or worst I've charted a new course,

to move forward in a different direction.

The Woman In Me

It's the woman in me that is so phenomenal,

that makes heads turn and mouths drop.

It's the woman in me that is so vulnerable,

that shutters at the thought of losing my heart.

It's the depth of my feelings that makes me sensational,

that touches the center of my core.

It's the nurturer in me that is so incredible,

it's the comforting presence you have grown to adore.

It's the soul in me that composes the melodies,

you hear whenever I speak my mind.

It's all the women that came before me,

that allows the woman in me to shine.

Love On My Mind

It entered my mind a time or two,

but this time it lingered in place.

I could no longer conceal what I felt inside

my feelings were written across my face.

My heart fluttered, my breath abated,

as I hesitated in pause to second thoughts.

Asking myself over and over,

"Will my love be enough?".

Hearts ablaze as passion fans the flames

of moments set adrift in my mind.

This time, when I bind my eyes,

I hope love is waiting on the other side.

With my eyes closed, dormant dreams

turn into vivid pictures of you and me.

Love blinds but to my surprise,

through closed eyes I can still see.

I want to release these lingering thoughts,

detach them and allow them to go.

Liberate myself from the tightening grip of love's captive hold.

Feelings evolve, expanding into vacant space, over the course of time.

Then turn into residual thoughts that leave love embedded on my

your mind.

Where Flowers Bloom

In the garden of the heart,

the place where love starts and flowers bloom.

Pick the flower you most admire and place it on a pedestal.

Admire the flower, but don't forget to shower it with love and care.

Savor the fragrance it releases when it blooms,

the fragrance that lingers in the air.

If you touch it, touch it softly,

ensure its delicate petals don't bruise or break.

When you speak, speak to it lovingly, say sweet words each and

everyday.

Provide your flower enriched soil, plant its roots in fertile ground,

adjust the temperature to tolerable, so it will bloom all year around.

As that flower grows its petals will glow colorful and bright.

The bloom of that flower will illuminate the room,

and forever be the light of your life.

It's In Me to Move This Way

It's in me to move the way I do.

The sway of my hips when rhythm slips between my thighs.

The glimpse from your eyes as I swoon from side to side,

leaving you mesmerized.

Were you surprised by the ancient rhythm I keep inside?

The music is the key to releasing the spirit and setting my soul free.

I close my eyes and extend my hand,

hoping to grasp the hand of the beat.

Each note I hear enters my ears and travels to my feet.

That ancient spirit inside of me

interprets the sound that sounds so sweet.

Inspired, I move in synchronicity

as the music moves through me.

Meanwhile the ancient voice inside my head

encourages me to dance, dance, dance.

One Last Kiss Upon Your Cheek

When the time comes to say goodbye,

and move on to whatever future is waiting for me;

it will be bittersweet.

The connection we share is strong,

but once happiness is gone,

then it is time to part ways and leave.

Leave you behind

in the piles of memories left spread across the floor.

Leave behind the one person in the world, above all others,

whom I most adored.

Though I am sad to let you go the future has already been spoken;

when love stops feeling like love those feelings turn into pain,

and leaves you feeling broken.

Let's share one last embrace, as we allow ourselves one last cry.

Come closer, so I can place upon your cheek my final kiss

as we say our last goodbye.

Puppetry

Pull my strings I will dance and sing,

move in ways you and ask me to.

Made of wood I will do as I should,

whatever it is you require me to do.

Look at me.

What do you see, beneath the splinters and carvings?

My hollow structure possesses no heart

nor soul inside this wooden body.

You attend to me as if you can't see

the strings attached to my hands.

The restrictions and fears, the endless tears,

that ceded control and command.

I will no longer be the puppet on the string,

dangling for all to see.

I'll cut the strings, break the rods,

and set myself free.

An unoccupied space with a missing face

will be all that's left of me.

My wooden self, will turn to flesh,

and I'll be free of your puppetry.

Beautiful Like Me

Don't you want to be, beautiful like me?

Look inside where my beauty hides,
before it blossoms for others to see.
Am I beautiful because of what you see on the outside,
or am I beautiful because of what's inside of me?

Inside each woman is the portal of life,
where she carries the seed from the root of the tree.
Where she bears the fruit the world needs,
and connects what begets adjoining legacies.

What you see on the outside of me,
may catch the glimpse of your eye.
Adorned in fashion, hairstyles that are spectacular,
glammed up and looking fly.
What I wear and what I bear, is all up to me.
Make no mistake I dress this way
because it reflects my personality.

I am beautiful in all phases, the definition of a lady,
I do it all so gracefully.
The question on my mind that I constantly want to ask is,
"Don't you want to be, beautiful like me?"

How Deep Does Beauty Reach?

How deep does beauty reach,
when viewed from the outside looking in?
How can it be measured,
when it lies deep beneath the skin?
How far does beauty extend
before it's recoiled or retracted?
Is the extent of beauty measured
by depth of color or blackness?

Is she beautiful for what she wears?
Is she beautiful for what she shows?
Is she beautiful because of her spirit,
or for what lies at her core?

It's not the hem of her skirt,
nor the length of her hair.
It's not her personal wealth
nor the clothes that she wears.
It's the way her presence fills the air
that makes her beautiful
and leaves you wanting more.

Un-tie Me

Emotionally, you tied me

to assumptions that simply weren't true.

Accused me of loving myself

more than I loved you.

Made me feel that it was something I did

that was pushing you away.

In reality, you took advantage of me

before taking your love away.

Why didn't I see

you no longer wanted me?

Why did it take so long?

How can it be, that you are always right

and I am always wrong?

I feel so lost.

Am I really in your heart?

It feels like I don't belong.

Un-tie me and set me free,

I am better on my own.

Sassy Chic

Excuse me,

did you just roll your eyes?

Did your attitude just cross paths with mine?

Did you just passively launch an attack at me,

by making a comment un-necessarily?

Were those your eyes I felt on my back?

Are you envious of how I wear my Black?

I think you would be jealous of any color, as a matter of fact.

If it is worn with pride, manicured to perfection.

Sassy and chic, and unpretentious.

Maybe if you put away the jealousy,

I will teach you how to be sassy and chic like me.

But don't let your lips bite off more than you can chew,

I have mastered being a diva, and I will use it if I have too.

Brave, Beautiful, and Bold

Can't you see, I am just being me,

the best me that I can be?

I don't have to be,

what you think I should be,

when I am so good at being me.

Hat to the side, when I walk I glide,

others quiver in my wake.

I wear my glory like a crown,

with my hair up or down,

and I love who I am.

Confidence running high,

my eyes focused on the prize,

spiritually I am feeling great.

Who knows what the future holds,

I just know I am brave, beautiful and bold,

and ready for whatever awaits.

The Prettiest Flower

The prettiest flowers grow in gardens where weeds are clipped away.

Where the soil is moist and fertile of course,

to nurture their growth each day.

Wild and free they are beautiful to see

in their splendid colors and hues.

There are many beautiful flowers in the garden,

but none as beautiful as you.

Once Again

Once again,

I can't erase from my memory the things I know.

Hurtful moments that haul me back to where I was before.

I wonder, is love really true?

Because, the only time love is good is when it's new.

Once again,

The cruelty of your love haunts me while I am lying in bed.

The chase for reciprocity runs through my head.

Replays of all the negative pictures looping in my mind.

Sometimes, love can be so unkind.

Fabulous

When I look in the mirror, what do I see?

A fabulous woman staring back at me.

Her beauty untouched by the sands of time,

her sun kissed skin the same as mine.

Her eyes scan beyond the image in the mirror,

beyond the past, present and future before her.

Her lips pursed, as if she is poised to speak,

to share words of wisdom to enlighten me.

I see her nearly everyday,

at the same time in the same place,

Perhaps she has something she wants to say;

"Excuse me Miss."

Yes?

"You look absolutely fabulous!"

When Love Leaves

Leaked secrets and personal thoughts never meant for others to hear,
creep pass in silence, to avoid awakening sleeping fears.

It's difficult to release the feelings when you're uncertain of which
direction they will go. Afraid that others will find out what you don't
want them to know.

Feelings fading, love abating, confined to the darkness of shadows.
Tears left traces upon our faces when they fell from our eyes long
ago.

Why are you always the forgiver, when I'm the one under attack?
Why do you implore me to give more love,
when you repeatedly take yours back?

We can't recapture the feelings and secure them back inside our heart.
The flame of passion extinguished, love forfeited at great costs.

Lying here looking at the ceiling, pondering how we got to this spot.
Wondering if any of the shattered pieces can ever be
re-attached.

Traveling in opposite directions,
far from where we use to be. I guess this is what it feels like,
when love decides to leave.

Uppermost

Up on high above the space where clouds form,

where crystalline skies give rise to clear thoughts,

and clear thoughts uncloak

to reveal your deepest thinking.

Where summits are aligned

in perfect formation.

The place where feelings connect

at the highest elevation.

Where the air becomes thin

and the pulse slows to cautious.

This is the place I reserve for you.

Atop the uppermost summits of my thoughts,

at the highest point.

Connect With Me

Connect with me.
Let me share with you who I am
Let me unlock my heart and escort you inside,
where my most passionate feelings reside.
Like a delicate flower sprouting from the ground,
I spread my arms and stretch.
Reaching for you, in hopes that we can connect.

Everything I desire I see in your eyes.
Even though you try concealing it from me, I still see,
the hollow spaces where love use to be.
Left barren and vacant, waiting to be refilled,
the deep wounds that only love can heal.

Connect with me,
and we can watch the stars light up the sky.
Share our visions of the life we will like to have.
We can chase our dreams through open fields,
and love each other with all we have to give.
Being with you is like a dream come true.
Connect with me.
My love is waiting for you.

Unzip Me

Unzip me, please.
Unleash the woman beneath the make-up and pretense,
uncover what is residing at the core of my essence.

I dwell,
beneath the outer shell,
Where I stare at the world through lenses,
colored by stereotypes and expectations,
that I, constantly fall short of meeting;
that scream "you are imperfect!"
So please, unzip me.

My arms can't reach far enough behind my back,
to ensure the zipper is on track before I pull it back
to release and reveal what it holds inside.

Are you ready to see me the way I am?
Are you ready to see me in my natural state?
Are you ready to accept my imperfections,
disregarding what others may think?

Are you ready,
to unleash the woman lurking beneath?
At the base of my nape, where my clothes start to drape
Come love, and unzip me.

Peel Back the Layers

I am complicated,
there are numerous layers that your eyes may not be able to see.
But, if you clear your mind and take your time you can peel back the
many layers of me.

Deep inside, where the soul resides, where dreams come alive,
and hope breathes its first breath of life.
In this place where I keep safe
my treasures from prying eyes.

Filled with pride, I attempt to hide the core of who I am.
I am willing to share if you promise not to tell
the condition you found me in.

My heart fractured and torn, was renovated and restored,
and now beats again.
I don't want to be alone; my feelings need a home;
a place where they can live.

When you finally find what I hide inside
you will see my feelings are sincere.
So with your tender touch, reach into my thoughts,
and peel back what the layers conceal.

Slip On My Baby Doll

I'll slip on my baby-doll,
look so good it will turn you on;
bring to life your every dream,
make real all your fantasies.

Give love unconditionally.
I have no time for misery.
I want someone who is into me,
who can provide their love faithfully.

Whatever you do don't hesitate,
show me the effort you are willing to make.
Embrace the sacrifice love extracts.
I'll reward your effort by loving you back.

My arms are waiting to hold you tight,
but only if you treat me right.
Open your heart, tear down the walls,
and I'll slip on my baby-doll.

Serenity

My mind is in a place

where chaos has been replaced by a calming peace.

No more trouble for now,

I can hear the harmonizing sounds of serenity.

Only moments ago I was feeling low

from the weight of everyday life.

Then something came over me ushering in a peace,

That made everything wrong right.

I heard the birds singing, and saw flowers bloom.

I felt a warm breeze passing,

dispensing nature's perfume.

In was in this moment of tranquility,

that I surrendered to the comfort of serenity.

I was finally in a place that I desired to be,

and for the first time in my life I felt completely free.

Feel Me

You think you can see everything you need to see from the outside
looking in? Look again.
My beauty lies beneath the skin, buried deep within.
Where I am most beautiful, your hands can't reach;
near the core of my essence next to my heart beat.
The place where I keep my secrets and desires away from prying eyes
and the cutting words of liars.

You need a key to open me, and I don't give them away.
To be welcomed into my heart you must have the intention to stay.
I am not interested, in temporary residents, who never buy; they
always rent. They leave places in need of repair, mark up walls, leave
cupboards bare. They move on never saying goodbye.
You look up one day and they're gone away, leaving you high and dry.

What I need is someone who feels me.
Someone who understands that what a woman needs lies in the touch
of their hands; the tenderness of their words; in the gentleness they
display only for her.

What I need is to feel secure,
like I am the princess they have been searching all their life for.
I need to know they will give anything in this world,
to make me feel loved like I have never felt before.

When I Was Your World

When I was your world nothing else mattered.
We would spend hours chatting;
talking about dreams that were still in the making;
talking about the mistakes we made while chasing
what we thought was love.

When I was your world together we,
explored the hidden spaces in the places we couldn't see.
Where thoughts hid away in secrecy,
in fear of their personal safety.

When I was your world I felt empowered.
I felt loved by you, and you,
felt loved by me too.
If only we could be that couple again,
and see the world through rose colored lenses.

When I was your world I definitively knew,
you were everything to me and I was everything to you.
Can we please go back to that time,
when I was your world, and you were mine?

Jealous Eyes

I have been told so many times that my star doesn't shine,

when seen through jealous eyes it's dimly lit.

With my head held high I walk right by

ignoring all the jealous eyed critics.

Why do they stare at me?

There must be something they desire to see.

Maybe they admire my presentation.

I glance briefly their way, smile and wave,

then walk away without hesitation.

Keeping my dreams alive, I continue to strive,

to be successful in my career, my relationships and love.

The next time those jealous eyes gaze upon me,

they will be dazzled by the star shining above.

Attitude

I don't possess an attitude,

but you best not mess with me.

If you want to play games; I am all about the victory.

You might think I'm pushy,

that merely shows you don't know me well.

I'm a refined lady,

but I'll unleash on you sheer hell.

I don't possess an attitude;

I just exude confidence.

I am clever and sassy, chic and classy,

it may put you on defense.

You might think you can handle me,

by setting me in my place.

But my words will flow as I let go

and paint my opinion all over your face.

It Could Have Been You

It started as a thought, but then turned into something else.

I wanted to be with you, to express the feelings that I felt.

You seemed to be indifferent,

as if my thoughts and feelings didn't matter.

The crack you heard, must have occurred

when my heart fell and shattered.

I merely wanted to hear the words,

"I love you!", spoken with sincerity.

I wanted to know the person I loved was still in love with me.

But instead the words "I love you",

remained trapped inside your mouth,

And when you gathered the courage to speak,

you swallowed, and nothing came out.

Laying here with my eyes wide shut,

trying to see clearly the pictures in my mind.

Reminiscing of moments past, when you laid asleep by my side.

I am certain another lover will occupy the vacant space,

once my memories of you fade, dissipating the outline of your face.

I will think about all the things that we did,

and the things we didn't do,

while clutching my new lover's hand,

knowing it could have been you.

Nude In Solitude

Sitting nude in solitude ensnared in the rapture of the moment after.

I feel divine, as if love unearthed what I was attempting to hide.

The intensity of passion,

unbridled roamed openly across my body's plane,

compelling me to answer pleasure's call with a scream.

Laying in the nudeness of now,

covered in the erotic fragrance created by two bodies discovering

synergy.

I melt inside of you as you absorb all of me.

Is this the beginning of unforgettable?

Is this our relationship's epic end?

Will I pay the ultimate price of remorse

for letting love back in?

For You

"What will you do for me?", she said to he.

He said to her, "I will always put you first."

She said to he, "Show me!" He said to her,

"For you, I would soar above the earth,

jump over the moon to capture a star,

and bring it back to your waiting arms.

For you, I would raid the sun,

steal its radiance and place it in your palms.

For you, I would swim the seas,

dive to depths no one has ever seen,

in search of pearls suitable for a queen.

For you, I would walk through fire,

across the embers of passion where love burns hottest.

For you, I would reach into your dreams,

gather all your fantasies and patch them into reality.

For you, I would explore every corner of the earth,

climb every mountain high, swim the depths of every sea,

and soar through every sky.

I would give all I own to make everyone of your dreams come true;

because there is nothing I wouldn't do for you!

The Last Rose

One rose fell from the dozen that you handed me,

landing gently on the bed.

We had just awaken,

and both our imprints could be seen where we last laid.

I wanted to remain where we were,

lying in each other's arms.

It was the place I felt most comfortable,

it was the place where I felt I belonged.

As I got up to put the eleven roses in a vase,

I left the one that fell lying on the bed.

Its sweet fragrance dispersed across the sheets,

and the thought of the sweet gesture

became a memory forever embedded in my head.

The moment brought me to a pause,

as I reflected on what transpired and was pleased.

I thought to myself,

how lucky I must be.

The person I love the most in this world,

just gave their last rose to me.

THE END

Nothing ever ends, it just changes,

pieces get rearranged and become strange to us;

fade away slowly until it disappears

and all that is left

is our fears,

and tears.

Want more copies?

Website: http://TimidMasses.com
Amazon: https://www.amazon.com

timid.masses@gmail.com

Made in the USA
Columbia, SC
10 February 2020

87758570R00055